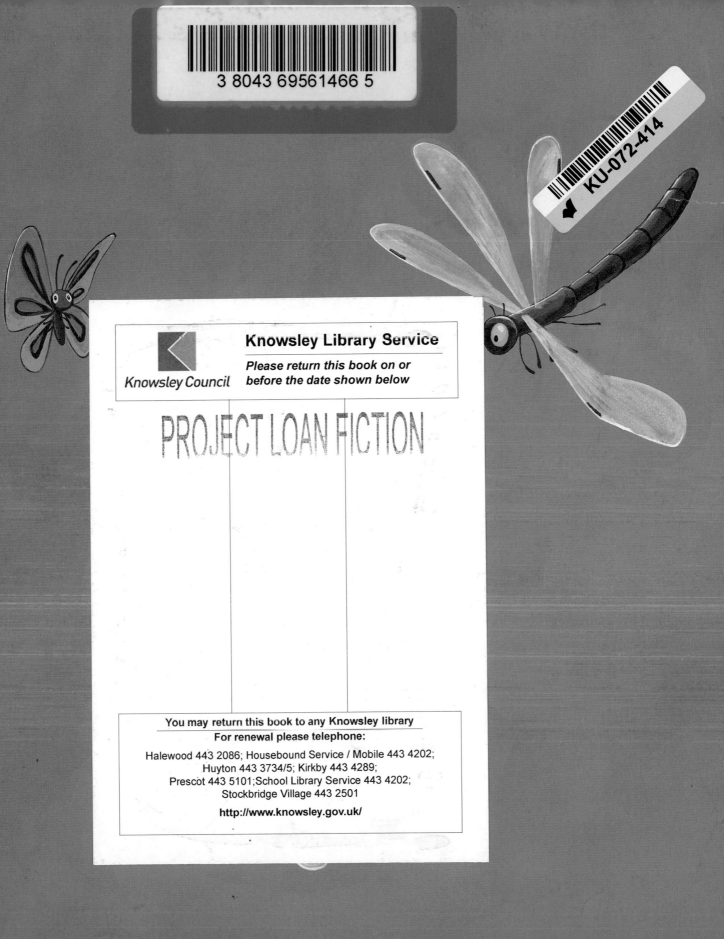

For Amelia – E B

For Lucy Louise – J C

LITTLE TIGER PRESS
1 The Coda Centre, 189 Munster Road, London SW6 6AW
www.littletiger.co.uk

First published in Great Britain 2014

ISBN 978-1-84895-743-5
LTP/1400/0746/0913

10 9 8 7 6 5 4 3 2 1

Elizabeth Bennett

Jane Chapman

Big

and Small

LITTLE TIGER PRESS
London

On a bright and sunny day, Big and Small go out to play.

Big

climbs high.

Small crawls low.

When suddenly, Small stubs his toe.

"A little help, please!" calls Small.

They cross a stream.
Jump, skip, hop, hop.

When **suddenly,**
Small **has** to **stop.**

"A **little** help, please!"
calls Small.

What's for **lunch?**

Hmmmmmm.

Let's see . . .

...When suddenly,
Small spots a bee!
"A little help, please!"
calls Small.

High on a

hill. What fun! Let's roll.

When suddenly,
Small's down
a hole.
"A little help, please!"
calls Small.

Back

home to bed.

They're warm
and snug.
But Big can't sleep –
he needs a hug.
"A little help, please!"
calls Big.